# The Billion Dollar Heir

## Book 1 in The Billion Dollar Series

## Sheila

DEDICATED TO
my readers

# CONTENTS

# ACKNOWLEDGMENTS

This book is for those of you who have read this and offered constructive criticism and great feedback. Thank you for your never-ending patience.

# Chapter 1

Tristan Devereux was a perceptive man. It was a trait he was blessed with at an early age. He knew when a clock wasn't ticking or when it ticked ahead or behind. He noticed how a crowd of people often split for him when he was in their presence. The women in his department offered him smiles and twirled their hair around their little fingers while the men pretended to enjoy every waking hour catering to his company. They only despised him for the success he created all on his own.

So, of course he knew this woman who was sitting across from him wasn't lying. Auburn hair, gray eyes and plump lips he had visualized every day since being apart from her.

"Pregnant," he said, the word rolling off his tongue like a curse word.

"Yes, Mr. Devereux, I am pregnant with your child." She cast her eyes down to her nails to avoid his intense hazel eyes. He noticed that immediately but wasn't fazed by it. "Anyway, you don't even remember me. I just thought you should know. Goodbye."

With those words dangling in the air, she stood up from her chair and fastened the buttons of her jacket. Her hand was on the door when Tristan suddenly said, "I want a DNA test and then I'll have you sign a confidentiality contract when you return with the results."

Those gray eyes flared with rage. Oh, yes, he remembered this one. The little virgin... which she never admitted to that night. She had been a challenge, and when he finally stumbled into bed with her, he didn't ever want to stop his deep thrusting or the desperate movement of her hands in his hair, pulling him closer and closer until they came together.

Her hands had fumbled, and her breath had quaked, but her lips were the only steady thing as he tasted the sweetest part of her.

But it was because of moments like these that made him doubt trust and people in general. There had been several women claiming to be carrying his child since he started his business in modern medicine. It happened to almost every man in the Devereux family as elite members of society.

"I refuse to take a DNA test," she said in utter disgust. "I was here to inform you about your child, but don't you worry because I'll be out of your life the second I walk out this door."

And it was the truth. Olivia couldn't even look after herself, so another human being was out of the question. She personally didn't believe in abortions, and it wasn't an option, especially with the guilt she was feeling just by thinking about it. She knew the facts, how pregnancies worked and how ending it worked. She worked in a hospital, but that didn't mean she couldn't have an opinion.

Once again, Tristan's voice stopped her. "You will take a test. We have a lab downstairs you'll go to so there will be no mix-ups."

She blinked hard at him, dropping her mouth in shock and disbelief. "I don't want anything from you. And you sure as hell don't want anything from me."

"Olivia," he said, drawing out her name the same way he had during their passionate night. "I want my child. Give me proof it's mine so I can take this predicament off your hands."

She laughed at the insensitive man, but there was no humor in what he was saying. "How dare you have the nerve to call my child a predicament? There is nothing unpleasant about the blood I carry. Goodbye, Mr. Devereux, and I hope you rot in hell."

He was amused by the way she had spoken to him, even after she had long disappeared behind his office door. She didn't want him in his child's life. He knew it was his, and if she was carrying his heir, there was no way he'd pass up an opportunity to know so.

"Jack," he spoke calmly to the man who stood at the door of his office. "Do whatever it takes to get me those results."

"Yes, sir."

It wasn't more than two hours later when Tristan managed to dig up Olivia Avery's entire life. While he waited for the results, he figured he could pass the time by getting to know the mother-to-be of his child.

She studied at the state university as a psychology major then went on to medical school where she was placed in one of the teaching hospitals he just so happened to own. She didn't even make half as much as Tristan did in an hour, but what intrigued him most was that he couldn't find a single thing on her family. Surely the woman had to have had someone looking out for her. But nothing came up in his search.

Then interest grabbed him again when he saw she was found off a highway as an infant. It was a wonder why she had no family listed. She truly was alone, but she was well off based on his research.

He grabbed his suit jacket hanging from his chair and pulled it on. It was taking Jack too long to do his job, so Tristan decided he would personally find out what he and the mother of his child should do about the situation.

"You'd think I want this baby," Olivia muttered as she looked down at the fussing infant. "Working with you little monsters is the highlight of my job, but what am I going to do when I'm called in out of the blue like this? My baby will need me."

Tristan admired her from behind the glass. When she wasn't home, he tried the hospital next, assuming she would be at work. The woman at the information desk had looked so pleased when he walked in until he asked for Olivia. There was no way of masking the look of disappointment on her face after that.

"I'm going to make sure you get a nice family who will love and protect you just like I will for my little baby." She smiled at the small prize in her arms, and for a moment, Tristan could see her speaking that way to their child. "You will have parents who smile at you even when you wake them up at four in the morning and big brothers who will love you more than they show with a little sister who looks up to you."

The child smiled at her, and it instantly brought light to Olivia's eyes. Tristan didn't miss it. It wasn't hard to catch such beauty in one person.

Clearing his throat, he stepped into the room and straightened out his suit jacket. Olivia set the infant back down into her incubator and immediately felt the presence behind her. It was the same suffocating presence from hours ago and the same one three months ago at a bar.

"You can't be in here," she said, not even bothering to turn around. "They're vulnerable in this state."

"My child won't suffer the way these children have to."

"Isn't your child lucky then?" she asked, rolling her eyes.

"Look at how precious they are. I wish I could take them all home and away from this."

"You're getting emotionally involved."

"It's something I'm working on," she muttered as she brushed past him and into the hallway. She just knew he'd follow. "How'd you find out where I work?"

"Take the test, Olivia." He stepped toward her when she stumbled against the wall but thought better of it and kept his distance. "That child is an heir to every asset I own. I will not let it be labeled illegitimate."

"And how do you plan to solve this problem, Mr. Devereux?"

He smiled at the very thought that crossed his mind multiple times on his way here. "You knew who I was that night—"

"I had no idea until I walked into the building to find your face plastered across every wall," she snapped, drawing in a sharp breath once she calmed down from her outburst. "Excuse me, Mr. Devereux, it's my lunch break and you of all people should know my child needs the proper nutrients."

"Our child," he corrected. "And because you asked, I am planning to resolve our child's illegitimacy through marriage. Shall we continue this someplace more private?"

Olivia was angry. Who did he think we was to waltz in and demand marriage? She was beginning to think confronting him about the pregnancy was nothing more than a mistake. Meeting him in the first place was a mistake. And standing before him was a mistake.

Once she had composed herself, Olivia stormed past the man and hurried off into an empty supply room. She jumped when she saw the familiar silhouette and laughed to herself once she realized who it was.

"I didn't think anyone was in here."

Aaron smiled at the woman. He absolutely adored her. She was always the little sister he never had. Born into a family with all brothers, it wasn't hard to fall in love with Olivia the moment he met her.

But of course, their feelings for each other never passed the boundaries of family. In fact, Aaron was the closest thing to family that Olivia had.

"You hiding from someone?" he asked, bringing a devilish smirk to his lips. "There are whispers going around that the famous owner Tristan Devereux is here in our hospital. I wonder who he's here to see."

"Why didn't you ever tell me?" She rolled her eyes when he stared impassively back at her. "You never told me who he was when I walked out of the bar with him."

He chuckled. "I assumed you knew."

"I've been in my own world for years," she murmured with the shake of her head.

"His face shows up in a small town, too, Ms. Oblivious."

Once again, she rolled her eyes and gently slapped his arm. "I told him about my baby. He wants to marry me."

"Well he has to go through me first."

Aaron stood at 6'3, just two inches shorter than Tristan based on what images she could conjure up in her mind. They had a similar build, but Olivia would put her money on Aaron to win in a brawl between the two men. He looked a little more beat up, coming from the inner city as a child while Tristan was too composed to even lift a finger.

But their night together proved otherwise. He worked wonders on her body, and she could never forget the way she came over his mouth, gripped the bed sheets for dear life, and even drew blood from his flesh. Tristan was composed, but he was not gentle.

"Wanna hide behind me?" Aaron asked, drawing her away from her wild thoughts. "Devereux won't look at me if I walk past him. You'll be safe."

Olivia nodded and reluctantly followed him out the storage room. Tristan wasn't in the hallway where she had left him, and she was thankful for that until a voice pulled her back. "Dr. Avery," the chief called. Reinhold was a scary grouch, but he had a soft spot for Olivia, considering she was the only person to make light of her living conditions while she was in and out of foster homes. He would have adopted her then, but he was just a volunteering doctor. He was more than just pleased to have her work at the hospital years later though. "Tell me exactly why Mr. Devereux here has not been attended to. He told me he paged you and asked to discuss adding a new department."

"Chief," she said, glaring at a very pleased Tristan, "I don't have a say or the voice to discuss adding new departments, much less one that Mr. Devereux–"

"I don't care, doctor. If he wishes to speak to you, you speak to him. The man owns every hospital in the state of–"

"It really wasn't her fault," Tristan piped in, suddenly guilty about the whole situation. "She doesn't have a voice as an attendee. I will speak to my construction team and see to that I have an office tomorrow morning."

"What?" Olivia and Aaron questioned simultaneously.

Tristan grinned in victory at the woman. "Darling, did I not mention you and I will be working side by side? Seeing you at home every night just won't cut it for me."

Reinhold's eyes widened in surprise. Since when was his little Olivia with the owner of practically every institution that practiced medicine? And why wouldn't she tell him? He was like a father to her, or so he thought.

"That's just wonderful," she muttered before angrily taking off again.

There just wouldn't be rest with Tristan Devereux in her life.

# Chapter 2

"You asleep?"

Aaron grunted when he felt the light tapping on his chest. "Go back to bed, Olive. This is the only sleep I'll be getting this week."

She pouted. She didn't mean to, but she did. Aaron instantly gave in, pulling her into his twin size bed and threw the comforter over them.

"I'm not here to sleep," she muttered, but she couldn't help but snuggle against him. "Tristan is in the living room."

"Now?"

"Yes now. Help me get rid of him."

The two entered the living room where Tristan had begun pacing back and forth. The place was not standard living off a pediatrician's salary. It was too... poor for his taste and hers.

"Why are you here?" Aaron asked as he and Tristan met the gaze of one another.

"I see you have company."

Olivia watched as his lips became a thin line. She couldn't understand Tristan's bitterness, but it wasn't like she understood him at all anyway.

"He's my roommate."

"Your roommate?" he repeated, rapidly shaking his head. "Your female friend is a roommate. Your sister is a roommate. Not this... here!"

Aaron's jaw clenched as he pulled Olivia behind him and balled his hands into fists. "Maybe I shouldn't leave you alone with him."

"You can head back to bed," she said, ignoring the deadly look on Tristan's face. "I'll handle this."

Aaron gave the man a warning glare as he turned back to his bedroom. Leaving his best friend alone to face the devil himself was stupid, but he knew Olivia was a smart girl.

Tristan circled around the living room. He didn't fit well in the place.

Olivia noted how it was too small for a man his height. It was also too small for Aaron, but she at least got used to seeing him in their home. Tristan, on the other hand, looked out of place.

"Your boyfriend?"

She looked up at him and shook her head. "He's a friend."

"Have you given any thought to my proposal?"

She crossed her arms over her chest. "It wasn't a proposal."

"What do you want?" he asked, fingering the ring in his pocket. He was beginning to think coming here was a bad idea. "Me on a bended knee with candles and petals? I'm not a romantic, Olivia. But I will do that if I have to."

"I don't want you to propose. I don't want you to do anything and" –She groaned when he dropped down on one knee and presented her with a diamond ring– "especially not that! Get the hell off my floor, Mr. Devereux."

"It's Tristan to you." He took a hold of her hand and slipped the ring on before she could pull away. "We'll be married this weekend at my parents' estate. Invite who you want and don't worry about the dress."

"I will not marry you," she said, angrily throwing the ring at him. "You cannot come into my life demanding I tie my life to yours. I will give you joint custody of my child–"

"*Our* child."

"But I will not be forced to marry you. Now get out of my apartment."

"Why did you come to me then?" he asked, suddenly angry at the stubborn woman. "You didn't come to me to kindly let me know you're carrying my child. You want something."

"I wanted the father to know he had a child out there," she snapped.

She ran a hand through her auburn hair in frustration and sighed, as if to calm herself down. "But you probably have a soccer team out there you're unaware of."

"Olivia–"

"Just get the hell out of here. I don't want to see you again."

He bitterly chuckled. "I'm not finished, Olivia. I will get

those test results and see to that this child has active parents in its life."

Tristan knew he wouldn't sleep tonight. He couldn't sleep, and he didn't know if the mother of his child was taking care of herself. If she wasn't, she wasn't caring for his child. He couldn't have that.

Which was his reason for insisting on marriage. He could care for her to know his unborn child was alright. But she had thrown the ring back in his face and refused.

He held the ring up to the light in his room and examined the platinum band. Was the diamond too small? Perhaps she preferred a golden band.

No, this was Olivia. She didn't dote on expensive items. She didn't even know Tristan was a walking bank when they had met at a bar and left together to his hotel room. That night was the best of all nights for him.

"Uncle Tristan!"

He knew that voice. He lived for it.

He felt the bed dip and laughed as he lifted the three-year-old, examining her beautiful and delicate features. "You're getting big, Lana. Where's your mom?"

She shrugged and collapsed beside her uncle, kicking off her shoes. "Mummy says you're sad and I should come make you happy."

He laughed at this. Ever since his youngest sister, Victoria, left for London four years ago with her husband, he had barely seen her or his niece. "Sweetheart, your uncle Tristan is only sad because you don't visit enough. You think Mommy will mind if I steal you away for a year?"

"I would miss Mummy!" she exclaimed, laughing wildly as he playfully poked at her. "But it's okay, Uncle Tristan, we're moving back with Granny and Grandpa."

He felt a rush of energy as he shot out of bed and carried her downstairs to his kitchen. He grinned when he saw his sister making herself at home and kissed her cheek. "You're really moving back?"

She casually nodded, as if she hadn't just returned from

London after four years. "Do you have any job openings at your office? Derek and I will be dirt poor until he finalizes his construction contract."

"I'll find you something," he murmured, pouring a cup of warm milk for his niece. "I'm stealing Lana, but you can have the guest room."

"Fine by me," she said, reading over the newspaper. "Derek and I haven't slept at all on the flight. Lana was out like a light so good luck."

It wasn't like Tristan had the ability to close his eyes and fall asleep anyway. He would stay up all night with the little girl if he had to.

There was a knock at the door when all was silent, and he wondered who could have been standing on the other side so late at night.

After settling Lana down on a kitchen stool, he made his way over to the door. His brows furrowed when he saw the woman behind the peephole and hurriedly unlocked the door for her.

"Olivia," he said, moving his eyes over her body. She had a pea coat wrapped around her with her arms crossed over her chest. He could tell she was cold and stepped aside to invite her in, but she didn't react to the gesture.

"I thought and thought about this all night," she blurted, throwing the speech she had prepared before coming over right out the window. She inhaled deeply, looked up at him and reached into her purse for a folded piece of paper. "I had the test done with your toothbrush I must have mistakenly packed that night. This child will be better off with both of us—"

She stopped when she saw the intrigued woman in his kitchen. Her dark blonde hair resembled Tristan's and so did the distinctive color of her hazel eyes. She was staring intently at Olivia, wondering who this woman was to her older brother as Lana watched with the same curiosity.

"You're busy," Olivia muttered more to herself. "I'm just... I'll go now."

Tristan shut the door behind them and followed her out into the hall, pulling her back by the arm. "If you have something to say, say it."

She dropped her gaze to the floor, but one finger hooked

beneath her chin and a look of desperation from him had her caving.

"People get married all the time and don't even love each other." She looked up at him and nervously bit her lip. "I don't want people thinking–I don't want them thinking anything about our child. So, if marrying you is what it takes, I'll do it. Just please keep the media out of it."

"I'm not God," he said, staring impassively at her. But inside, he was bursting with new energy. "But I will try, Olivia. I will protect our baby."

She smiled at the man and absentmindedly pressed her mouth to his, but it wasn't anything like the kisses they had shared their one night together. Blushing, she stepped away and dusted his shoulder. "I'll see you around, Mr. Devereux."

"Tristan," he corrected with a sly grin as he reached into his pocket and slipped the ring on her rightful finger. "And I'll have your things moved in first thing tomorrow morning."

"Don't push it."

# Chapter 3

"Ms. Edwards, your baby isn't stable enough to breathe on her own."

The woman fell into a heap of tears, and Olivia immediately felt her heart ache for her. She would be heartbroken if anything happened to her baby, considering the past week that had given her time to bond with the little speck inside her.

"We will be monitoring her closely through the night." Olivia reassuringly touched her shoulder and gave her a rueful smile. "You need to rest. Your baby will be just fine."

Tristan was right outside the room filling out paperwork when she stopped beside him and dropped her head in her hands. "Bad day?"

She shook her head. "I need to go home and have a hot long bath."

"You're really giving me an image there," he mumbled under his breath, but she chose to ignore it.

There was no doubt that her hormones had been giving her sinful thoughts. They mostly started with a very naked Tristan and always ended with her screaming his name as he made her cum over and over again.

It didn't help that he always wore button ups that she yearned to rip apart with her teeth. And she didn't know when his very presence became such an overwhelming feeling of sexual tension.

He licked his lips when he caught her staring at him. Her gray eyes were dark with lust, and he couldn't deny he felt some sort of sexual desire for her. He'd felt it the very night they met and even more so when she waltzed back into his life.

"Are you doing anything?"

She raised a brow. "Going home to take a hot bath."

"Do it at our place," he said, casually shrugging when she

snorted. "You'll have no choice but to live with me after our wedding this weekend."

Olivia cleared her throat and glanced around at the attention they had drawn. But no one was looking at her. They were all focused on Tristan, especially the whispering women.

"Who was that woman at your apartment the other day?" she asked, choosing to change the subject.

"My sister and her daughter. You want to meet them?"

She wanted to so she would have a familiar face at the wedding with his family, but she shook her head instead and turned to leave.

Aaron was in the locker room when she got there and stripped out of her clothes to change. He glanced at her, chuckling when she struggled to pull on her jeans.

"I'm getting fat and stretching in places I won't be able to see soon."

He laughed again. "You're barely five months along. And you are not fat. Come here, Olive."

She threw her shirt on and stepped toward him, wallowing in the comfort of his chest as he held her. "Do I tell you I love you enough? I don't tell you and now I'm getting married to a man I don't love. You will be there for the wedding, right?"

He nodded and silently stood still. He couldn't picture a life without her but knew he'd have to now that she was getting married. He knew she'd find a man to sweep her off her feet one day. Olivia was a beautiful woman, no lie. But he felt sorry for her to know she couldn't marry off to a man who loved her.

"Take me home," she said after a while.

It was late when they got to the apartment. Olivia immediately claimed the bathroom while Aaron went straight to bed. And of course, Tristan had followed her home to make sure she was alright.

He finally found the courage to go up to her apartment after an hour of sitting in the car and knocked on the door. Aaron opened it, took one glance at him and groggily pushed the door wider to let him in.

"Lock it behind you," he said as he returned to his room.

Tristan quickly locked the door and followed the sound of running water to the bathroom. He found that it was unlocked, entered and then dropped down on the balls of his feet beside

Olivia.

He ran a hand through her hair and moved on to trace her lips that were turning purple. "If you're trying to drown yourself, you're doing it wrong."

She swatted his hand away, turned off the water, and allowed him to carry her to bed. She was shivering without the warmth of a towel, but Tristan's body temperature was comfortable enough. "What are you doing here?"

"I'm making sure my fiancé is safe," he simply told her, leaving out the stalking part. "How long have you been in there?"

"I don't know," she murmured into the pillow when her head fell against it. She was completely naked, completely vulnerable to him, but he was her fiancé after all. "Don't drive back this late. Come sleep."

There was no way he could sleep in the same bed with her and do just that. But it was totally worth the risk when she touched his hand and drew it to her mouth to kiss it.

"Just stay," she whispered – her breath warm against his skin.

He pulled away and quickly undressed. He was respectfully in his t-shirt and boxers when he climbed into her bed. The last thing he expected was for Olivia to snuggle against him and run her hand underneath his shirt, caressing his abdomen in small circular motions. It felt comforting and foreign to him. It was affection in a new light.

"I know you followed me home. Usually, that would be weird, but you only had good intentions." Her hand paused when the two of them fell silent. Then it was moving again but closer to his thumping chest. "Goodnight, Tristan."

He chuckled and leaned forward to kiss her forehead. "Goodnight, Liv."


"That" –Beth pointed to the screen and smiled at her colleague– "is just a little part of you. It'll take a while until you start showing."

"I work here," Olivia reminded Beth. "And I'm certain my baby is growing inside me."

Tristan stopped mid-step when he saw the screen from the hallway and rushed to Olivia's side. "That's our child?"

Beth's eyes widened in surprise as she swiveled in her chair to turn to the screen. "You're the father, Mr. Devereux?"

As a proud father, he nodded and instinctively kissed Olivia's forehead. The gesture would have made anyone believe they were a couple in love, save for Beth who knew Olivia didn't believe in such sentimental endings.

"I'll give you a list of vitamins you should be taking in your second trimester," she said, glancing at Olivia who was admiring the small bump on her stomach. "You're sixteen weeks along and look perfectly healthy."

Tristan hadn't torn his eyes away from Olivia even when he knew he should to look at the ultrasound, but he was too caught up in the mother of his child to care about anything else. "Do you need anything? You're growing and should be wearing more comfortable clothing."

Olivia took his hand in hers and shook her head, smiling at the man who looked like he could be less bothered by a child when she first went to him. "I'll be fine, especially in our new apartment where I can take hot long baths."

"When'd you change your mind?" he asked, ignoring the curious glances they got from Beth.

"When my fiancé drove to my apartment just to see me off to bed," she whispered, lifting her head to kiss the corner of his mouth. "And when he stayed the night. I felt safe, Tristan."

He smiled at this and on instinct cupped the back of her head to pull her closer. "I'll always keep you and my child safe. I swear on my life."

"Marriage?" Victoria laughed at the idea and went back to reading her book. But she was still intrigued with the conversation with her brother and couldn't seem to return to her book. So, she set it down instead. "The woman is pregnant and you want to marry her? Is it even yours?"

"I've seen the DNA results," he said, rubbing the stubble across his jaw. "The baby is mine. There's no way I'm letting that child grow up without a father."

"Because you know the horrors," she mumbled. "We have a loving family with parents who love each other."

"Parents who love each other," Victoria repeated, laughing at the words. "Mum and Dad survived their marriage this long because they love each other. Do you even love your child's mother? You two won't last a year."

Olivia had heard enough for one night. She threw a pillow over herself and tried to drown out the voices in the living room. What was she thinking by moving in with Tristan?

His sister was right. They'd never last. The only reason why she was in Tristan's life was because of the life growing inside her. If she weren't carrying an heir to all his assets, he would have kept her buried in the back of his closet like the other women.

"Are you trying to hurt yourself?"

Olivia threw the pillow aside and smiled at the little girl she had met earlier. "Didn't Uncle Tristan tuck you into bed?"

She nodded. "But I like sleeping with Uncle Tristan and now you're in here."

Olivia ruefully smiled and patted the space next to her. "You can sleep here."

"My uncle really likes you. Maybe he wants you to be in his room."

She shook her head at the little girl and instinctively rubbed her baby bump. "It's late, Lana. You should sleep so a little girl like you can grow tall and healthy."

Lana grinned at Olivia and happily tucked herself in. "Goodnight, Olive."

Olivia laughed. Only one person called her Olive, and she was beginning to miss him. "Goodnight, sweetie."

Olivia quickly changed into a pair of jeans and a comfortable sweater before heading downstairs. Victoria and Tristan seemed to have moved their conversation elsewhere so sneaking out wasn't hard to do.

She glanced at the engagement ring on her finger and exhaled when she realized that she and Tristan were still engaged even if she took off. Reaching into her back pocket to make sure the key to her apartment was still there, she hailed a cab home. There was no way she would sleep in the same place with a woman who already seemed to hate her and a man who only kept her around for their child.

Olivia fumbled with the key once she got there and turned on the lights. There was noise coming from Aaron's room, and she could only guess he had company so she sat down in front of the TV. Seconds later, Aaron stumbled out to find his friend sobbing like she never did and settled down beside her, pulling her into his arms.

"Did he hurt you?"

She shook her head and found comfort in him immediately. "I can't do this. I can't be a mother and marry a man I don't love. This is all too much for me."

He didn't say anything as he allowed her to cry. Olivia Avery barely shed a tear, but it was a relief to him when she did because he knew she wasn't completely closed off.

"Is she your girlfriend or something?"

Olivia turned to the voice and quickly wiped her tears when she saw the woman standing naked before her. Her jaw fell unhinged and she turned to the floor. "I interrupted something. I'm gonna head to bed. Goodnight, Aaron."

She hurried off to her room and couldn't help the laugh that escaped her. Aaron sure knew how to pick women.

It was midnight when Tristan finally went upstairs for bed. He was surprised to find Lana fast asleep in his bed with no sign of Olivia. He checked every room and bathroom only to find that she was gone. But the luggage she packed was still in his room where she left it. And her phone was sitting on the nightstand.

Tristan immediately knew she hadn't just disappeared. She was back at her old apartment.

He quickly ran for his car downstairs and drove to find Olivia. Why would she up and leave when she had told him with certainty that she'd move in? Why did she run?

It had started raining on his way over, but he didn't care as he ran to the door and buzzed her apartment number. He was granted access instantly and continued to sprint upstairs. He knocked on the door, but no one answered. So with frustration, he continued banging.

Olivia knew that angry knocking was Tristan. Aaron's company had left almost an hour ago so they stood staring at each other and had a silent argument about who should open the door. Olivia lost when Aaron ran into his room to lock himself in, so she was forced to face the man alone.

But she stopped as soon as the knocking did.

"Olivia," Tristan defeatedly said. "I can't leave. I can't leave because if I do, it'll be because I don't care about the mother of my child. And I do care, otherwise I wouldn't want anything to do with this child."

Her breath hitched, and she could barely breathe as she looked through the peephole to see a worn-out Tristan. "Are you sane? I won't open this door if you're still angry."

He laughed, but even Olivia could hear the pain behind it. "I'm completely insane, Liv. I drove out here for you. I forced you to do things because it's the right thing. You fought me, but I fought, too."

She opened the door and was immediately met by hungry lips. She was too weak to fight or question what he was doing, so she wrapped her arms around his neck and allowed his tongue to taste her mouth.

Tristan kicked the door behind him as he pushed her into her bedroom. He was done resisting this woman's body. They were engaged for God's sake.

Olivia seemed to have wanted this just as much as he did. She was already working on his jeans with shaking hands. Perhaps when she wasn't too tired she could rip them apart. But for now, she would explore the depths of their pleasure.

She moved on to his t-shirt and pulled it up halfway until Tristan stepped away to lift it over his head. But he was more eager to have Olivia's naked body squirming beneath him. He only briefly touched her skin as he pulled her shirt off, but it was enough to have her dripping into her panties.

She kicked off her jeans and gasped in surprise when he hoisted her around his hips, throwing her onto the bed. His lips teased the corner of her mouth then lowered it to her jaw. She was already gasping for air by the time his mouth felt the soft curve of her breasts. He hastily unclasped the front of her bra and let it fall as he latched onto an erected nipple, tasting her and watching the pleasure on her face.

He pushed her legs apart and moved on to kiss her core. He could already feel how soaked her panties were, but just the sight of her would have him exploding.

Olivia felt her panties slide off and instinctively closed her legs, but Tristan pulled her knees apart. The lips of her pussy were wet just the way they were the night they had been together. All he had to do was touch her and her entire body was his. His tongue slid over her clit, earning a quivering moan from her mouth just as her hands fumbled through his hair.

Her eyes rolled back, and she could only surrender to the pleasure as his mouth completely devoured what he had longed to taste. She lifted her hips, rolled it against his tongue and released a series of sharp breaths. "Tristan, please..."

His tongue moved quick, flicking and circling around the most sensitive part of her. He hummed, and it sent a vibration through her spine that curved off the mattress. "Please what, Olivia?"

"Please," was all she could manage when he slid a finger into her dripping pussy. She became completely motionless against the bed and covered her mouth with her hand, letting the screams die in her throat.

Just as the pressure in her core built up and the tension in her body began to rise, he pulled away from her, kissing her inner thigh.

"Let's go home," he said, buttoning up his jeans. He reached for his shirt off the floor and pulled it on.

She gaped at him and in embarrassment reached for the comforter to cover herself. He noticed the look of horror in her eyes before she could express it and pulled her out of bed, pressing his lips to hers.

He broke away, caressed her cheek and offered her a smile. "I'm not finished yet, Olivia."

# Chapter 4

Something about her past brought her back.

It wasn't much of a highway. It was just an abandoned road now. And even though she had no memory of the storm or the passersby that night, being that child abandoned on the side of the road wasn't something to forget.

"I'd never leave you," she whispered to her baby bump. "Your Mommy and Daddy will give you a lovely home with lots of love. You'll never have to be alone."

Reinhold watched the woman from his car before stepping out. He often visited the site where he found Olivia as an infant. But he never once saw her around. Curious as to why, he walked over to where she aimlessly wandered around and called out to her.

She looked up with a small smile and clutched her jacket close to her. "Good morning, Chief."

"Is this why you called in today?"

She casually shrugged. "I didn't think I'd end up here. I forgot the story."

He offered her a smile and hooked her arm through his. He had told her the story of how he saved her from the storm many times as a child. "I still believe it was fate that brought us together. My car broke down, and I'd already had such a rough day at the hospital. I thought I was imagining those cries. You were just this tiny thing tucked in a shoebox."

"You're the only reason why I didn't go crazy."

He chuckled. There were times when he had considered adopting her. One day, he finally did go through with it. He had filled out the paperwork, waited for a hearing and waited to bring her home as his daughter, but the state always denied him. She was just a project, the ward who was untouchable because her story was too unique.

That was the reason why he always staying so close to her.

He never wanted her to stray too far. He had found her. He was meant to protect her, but she was getting married. She had someone else to do the job.

"I love you," she told him. She waited for the words to settle and wrapped her arms around his middle. "Thank you for everything."

Reinhold didn't have time to react because there was a car pulling up in front of them, distracting Olivia. Tristan stepped out and walked over to them, but he was only focused on his fiancé.

She accepted the kiss he gave her and mumbled a hello before pulling away.

"Are you alright?" he asked.

She nodded, and Reinhold instantly took that as his cue to walk elsewhere. "What are you doing here?"

Tristan shoved his hands into his pockets to keep them from shaking and chuckled to himself. "You have got to stop disappearing on me, Olivia. And I know I should stop worrying all the time, but I don't want anything happening to our child... or you."

The past few weeks with Tristan hadn't been the easiest. But the two had grown to tolerate each other. Until a few nights ago when the sexual tension suddenly became a thick cloud over them. Neither one of them had acted on it since then.

"I'm fine," she said, kissing him softly on the lips. Some time ago, affection had become a thing between them, and neither one of them seemed to mind. "And our baby is fine."

"What are you doing out here?" he asked, recognizing the place as the highway she was left on. It should have even haunting, but she really did seem fine.

"Reminiscing."

He chuckled and took her hand in his, stroking her knuckles with his thumb. "You can always do that with me. You never have to be alone, Olivia."

She smiled at this and instantly felt her heart stutter. "I told our baby almost the same thing. We may not love each other, but we'll love our child."

Tristan cleared his throat when he realized he was staring at her. Olivia was a beautiful woman, and she was even more beautiful to look at. He wasn't ashamed to admit it.

"We have to get down to my parents'," he said, cutting through the silence. "We can leave now and have more than hours of rest before the wedding."

Olivia wordlessly followed Tristan to his car and waved a goodbye to Reinhold. He gave the couple a brief nod but ran to the passenger side of Tristan's car before they could drive away.

"I won't be able to leave until late afternoon," he said to Olivia. "But I'll make it in time for your wedding."

She smiled gratefully at him and pecked his cheek. "Walk me down the aisle."

A smile plastered across his face as he nodded. "I'd be happy to walk you, sweetheart. Have a safe trip."


It was only noon when they arrived at the place Tristan called home growing up. His mother, Daphnia, greeted them at the door and kissed her son before giving Olivia a long embrace.

Victoria was in the kitchen, working on lunch with Lana when she took one glance at Olivia and sighed. "I know you heard Tristan and me talking. It was nothing personal because I genuinely love my new sister in law."

Olivia smiled and was instantly attacked with a hug from Victoria. She could barely breathe when she felt another pair of arms around her.

"She's even more beautiful in person," the woman said. "I'm Sadie, and I believe Stephen is eager to–"

"Did someone call me?"

Olivia was engulfed once more but found it oddly comfortable. She had never had so many people want to see her, especially people she would soon call family. "And you must be Stephen."

"Tristan bringing a girl home," he said, chuckling. "I had to see for myself."

Tristan entered the kitchen then. It was as if he could sense the unsettling nerves in his fiancé and stood beside her, kissing her hair to show her comfort and support.

"There's still Connor and Joseph you have yet to meet," he whispered.

"You're joking."

He shook his head. "Here they come. They're just as crazy as everyone else."

"*La sœur!*" Connor exclaimed before taking her from their brother's hold.

"I'm Joseph," the taller man said, kissing her hand. "*Elle est belle.*"

Her brows furrowed in confusion.

"Very beautiful," the other man said. He stood two inches shorter than Tristan and Joseph but was taller than the other brother Stephen. "And I'm Connor."

Tristan took Olivia's hand and pulled her back to his side, affectionately wrapping his arms around her. "They aren't too bad, are they?"

"And you fit in where?"

"Right after Connor," he said, admiring his siblings who couldn't keep their eyes off their brother's new prize. "Sadie here is the oldest. Much like you, she's very stubborn about marriage."

Olivia suddenly couldn't breathe. She couldn't believe he'd say that, especially in front of the people she would spend the rest of her life with. She pried her fiancé's arms away and stormed outside for a breath of air. It probably caused a scene, but fresh air was what she needed.

"Not cool," Connor said, shaking his head. "You can't blame her for not wanting to marry you. You knocked her up."

"How do you even know about that?" he asked, eyeing each of his siblings. "You told them, Victoria?"

"I told them," Kaine said, stepping into the kitchen. He frowned when Olivia was nowhere to be found. "It takes a lot to step up and be a father. But it's a man who stays. Your brothers and sisters should be proud."

"That he got a girl pregnant and forced her to come here?" Sadie asked, smiling innocently when Tristan glared at her. "We're so proud."

"You're judging her," Tristan said, glancing at the door Olivia had disappeared through. "Stop because that is the mother of my child you're talking about."

"They're judging *you*," Daphnia said to her son. "It was you who wrongly used your words. Now go apologize before I make you sleep in a hotel room without Olivia."

He was just about to step outside when the door was pushed opened with force. Olivia stood there with wide eyes before collapsing in his arms. Tristan shouted for his siblings to call an ambulance when all Olivia felt was the blood that ran down her leg.

This was not happening to her. Not now when all she could bear was having this child.


"It was just some minor bleeding," the doctor assured her. "You did not miscarry like you feared."

Olivia covered her face in her hands and rubbed the red color she couldn't stop seeing out of her eyes. "What is happening to me?"

The woman patted her shoulder and turned to the window that gave them a view of Tristan and the rest of his family. "Have you been stressed lately? Sometimes stress clouds your mind. Maybe more rest and eliminating the stress factors will help."

The stress was her fiancé and the wedding and moving away from her best friend and working late and everything that had piled up since she fell pregnant. Her life was well sorted and organized before Tristan came along.

But she couldn't blame all her stress on him because he was also part of the reason why she wasn't so stressed all the time.

"Can you call my fiancé into the room?" she asked the doctor.

She nodded at Olivia and glanced at Tristan from behind the glass. He stood frozen for a moment then finally made his way in when the door was held open for him.

Tristan desperately kissed Olivia and cupped her face in his hands, inhaling deeply as he pulled away. "Is everything alright with the baby?"

"You need to stop," she said quietly. "Stop worrying all the time because it makes me worry. And don't... say things like

I'm against marriage because that is not true. If I were, I'd be running for the hills right now. What I'm really against is marrying a man I don't love. And I'm so stressed and tired right now that—"

His mouth claimed hers before she could finish. Her argument died in her throat as she fisted his dark blonde hair and twisted it in her hands, desperately pulling him closer as he moved on to kiss her neck.

"You could have just told me you've been stressed," he mumbled against her skin. "I would have easily solved that problem with you, me, and a bed."

"Oh, God," she whispered when she felt the pressure of his erection against her. "Not now, Tristan. Your family is looking at us."

He turned to the window where he could tell that not a single member of the family was amused. Affection was normal for them, and showing it was just as normal. Even Tristan was beginning to accept that.

"We're going home," he said, helping her down from the exam table. "We'll get married tonight as planned and then I'll get rid of some of that stress for. Then we can go on that honeymoon of ours."

"You planned a honeymoon?"

He nodded. "This is a real engagement and wedding and marriage. I'm taking you on a honeymoon where I can help eliminate more of that stress."

She kissed him then followed him out into the waiting area. Victoria looped her arm through hers and reassuring rubbed her back, whispering comforting words to her sister in law.

"*Tu es amoureux*," Joseph said to Tristan as they all walked outside. "Holy shit, brother. You love her."

# Chapter 5

It wasn't a fancy cathedral. It was the backyard of the Devereux residence. But somehow, Tristan managed to turn the place upside down and made it beautiful for his bride. Joseph wasn't wrong when he exclaimed that Tristan was in love with Olivia. How couldn't he love a woman who put up a fight for herself and her baby? How couldn't he love a woman as beautiful as Olivia? How could he have not loved Olivia the moment they met?

It was crazy what love was to a world so cruel. It was crazy that it even existed between two people. He'd seen love live among a wonderful family like his, but experiencing it himself was completely different.

Olivia slipped Tristan's white gold wedding band on with shaking hands and blushed when she looked up to find that he was already staring at her.

"You're beautiful," he whispered just as the priest gave him permission to kiss his bride.

He cupped the back of her head with one hand and slipped his other arm around her waist, memorizing the touch of her lips against his as he kissed her for what he wished could be eternity.

They walked arm and arm down the aisle to the party table where Olivia took a seat between her husband and Aaron.

He leaned over to kiss her cheek and backed away with his hands raised when Tristan sent him a glare. "She's all yours, Devereux."

Olivia laughed and reassuringly took Tristan's hand under the table. Reinhold took a seat on the other side of Tristan and gave the couple a smile.

"My son," Kaine said into the microphone, "has done me proud by marrying such a beautiful young woman with a wonderful heart. Welcome to the family, Olivia."

Olivia leaned over to kiss Tristan. It felt like a show to him, but being in love was not a show. "This does feel like a real wedding."

"It is a real wedding," he reminded her, nuzzling her neck.

The night went on with excitable chatter, slow dancing and even a few intimate moments between the couple. Everyone genuinely believed they were in love, and Tristan wished that were true.

Olivia and Aaron were dancing when Tristan set down his drink and pulled Lana to the dance floor.

He kept his gaze trained on his beautiful wife and even more so when she disappeared behind other dancing couples.

"Aunt Olive looks like a princess," Lana said, admiring the bride. "Do you love her?"

"I do." He watched as she swayed across the dance floor with Aaron.

Aaron noticed the man's intent stare on his best friend the entire night and finally commented on it. "He hasn't stopped looking at you since you walked down the aisle."

Olivia laughed, as if it was the most bizarre thing to hear. "He's probably afraid I'll slip and hurt the baby."

"It isn't just the baby he cares about," he said, looking down at the clueless woman. "Have you ever considered that it might not be just about the baby?"

"The baby comes first. That was the deal."

"Deals can be broken when feelings come to play."

Olivia glanced at Tristan and smiled when she saw he was already looking at her. She wanted to be ravished by his hands in that moment. She wanted to feel him pulsate inside her, pounding and moving hard but gentle. She wanted him to make love to her and for him to love her.

This realization drilled into her mind and had her eyes dropping to avoid his gaze. She looked at an imaginary spot on Aaron's shoulder, fighting the grin on her lips as she came to accept this sudden confusion.

"May I dance with my wife before the night ends?" Tristan asked, extending a hand to Olivia.

She kissed Aaron's cheek before taking her husband's hand. It was warm and comforting. "I want to try tonight."

He quirked a brow at her. "Try what, baby?"

She swooned at the endearment but blushed when she realized she'd have to further explain words that weren't meant to come out so rash. "We're married now. Do we have to…"

Tristan suddenly realized what she was asking for then chuckled, leaning forward to kiss her lips. Her innocence was too pure. "I pictured somewhere a little quieter where I can hear you moaning right in my ear instead."

She shuddered at the thought but couldn't keep her mind away from those images. "We'd just have to sneak away."

He looked around and figured his guests wouldn't miss the couple too much if they disappeared. He took Olivia's hand and pulled her to the house in a slow, steady and casual manner. There was absolutely no way he would be taking his hands off her anytime soon.

They made it up to his room when Olivia hurriedly closed the door and pushed her husband against it, claiming his mouth with her own. Tristan had already started working on the zipper of her dress, but his hands moved slow, as if to savor every moment.

Her hand moved along the bulge in his pants, and he groaned. He caught her hand, bringing it to his chest where she immediately worked the buttons of his shirt. As much as Olivia wanted this man to throw her onto the bed and taste every inch of her body, she forced her hands to slow down and traced the outline of his naked torso, admiring the way his navel pulsed as he heavily breathed against her neck.

Finally, Tristan managed to pull her dress down and hummed in appreciation when he saw the lace material of her lingerie. "My wedding gift?"

She ran her hands up his body and cupped his face, pulling him in for a kiss. "Not exactly."

She dropped down in front of him and kissed his navel, trailing her lips further down until she reached his cock and took it into her hand. Reliving the images from their first night together, she licked the tip of it, circling her tongue against the flesh until he was slowly thrusting into her mouth.

The wedding band pressed against his flesh, and before she could completely wrap her mouth around him, he pulled her off the floor and onto the bed instead. Her ring was a reminder that they still had guests who'd wonder where the bride and groom had run off to.

Tristan caressed her cheek with the pad of his thumb and grinned. This woman was his to keep and love. It didn't matter to him that she didn't share his mutual feelings. All that mattered was that she was his.

He kissed her gently like the delicacy she was. Every part of her body would be covered by his lips, claimed by him and meant for him. His mouth moved down her shoulders, between the curves of her breasts and over her navel. There was something between them—a creation that had bonded them.

His lips grazed her inner thigh where her flesh was the smoothest and most comforting to rest between. With shaking hands, he pulled her panties down past her legs and threw it onto his suitcase across the room. He would be keeping those as a memory of their wedding night.

His tongue felt the lips of her pussy first and then the erect clit where one touch could make her shudder and moan. He longed to tease her to the depths of pleasure, but the longing look on her face and the swelling of his cock told him being buried inside her would be much more sensational.

He positioned himself against the entrance of her pussy, sliding the tip over her clit before thrusting inside. Olivia bit the back of her hand fought the gasps of pleasure as she tried to adjust to him.

Tristan wasn't breathing. He was looking down at the woman he had just married, the same one who carried his flesh and blood. He couldn't have possibly been so lucky. As if she could sense his moment of hesitance, she cupped his cheek in her hand and smiled reassuringly.

He blinked and withdrew just enough to feel the pressure of her walls grab him, refusing to release him. Every stroke felt as if she couldn't let go, and neither could he. There was something about the intimacy they shared and the beating of his chest against hers. They had married into that intimacy.

His hand moved to her neck where he stopped for a moment then she closed his fingers around her, granting him permission to do as he pleased. He was gentle with her just like the night they had met.

He didn't know how he maintained self-control around this woman for so long, but he wouldn't have to anymore. He could have as many moments like this as he wanted.

The bed creaked beneath them, and Olivia squirmed from underneath, wrapping her arms around his neck as he pulled her even closer to his body. He didn't want to let her go in that moment.

"Tristan..." she whispered.

His hands buried in her hair, and he pulled her closer until he realized their bodies couldn't be joined as one. Her pussy clenched around his cock, and before he could process what was happening, she'd already managed to drain every bit of him as his fingers sank into her flesh. He didn't say anything. He couldn't when she had taken control of every part of his body.

He kissed her for what felt like hours and refused to pull away. He didn't want to lose this contact. He didn't want to lose what they found here. What he found here.

Olivia heard the footsteps in the hallway first and quickly drew the blanket over them just as someone barged into the room.

"Damn," he said, eyeing Olivia. "I was hoping to catch you two in the act."

A smile spread across Tristan's lips when he saw who stood in the doorway. "Foster, just like you to show up when the party's over."

# Chapter 6

Olivia was picking at a piece of cake in the backyard at the party table. No one even noticed that the bride and groom had disappeared at one point, but everyone noticed when it was just the groom who came up missing. She couldn't count the number of people who had asked where he was hiding.

But it was Killeen Foster who showed up and snatched her husband away. Now the two of them were in the kitchen drinking beers and acting like this wasn't a wedding.

"Where's your husband?" Kaine asked, lifting his camera to snap a picture of the beautiful bride who wasn't smiling anymore.

"Somewhere around here with his friend."

Kaine seated himself across her and took the fork away. She needed a distraction, and destroying her wedding cake wasn't one.

"Killeen showed up," he said. He chuckled when she nodded. "He's Tristan's best friend. Always has been since they were children running around back here. My son becomes an idiot when he's around."

"He left me for him," she muttered. "My husband ditched me for his best friend."

He took her hand in his and ruefully smiled. "Olivia, I know you two don't love each other. But do you think you will with time? It worries me that my son thinks marriage is an answer."

"I honestly don't know," she truthfully said. "At least he values his family."

"That much is true."

"I think I love him," she murmured, turning away. She blushed when she realized what she had said and cast her eyes down to her wedding band. "I mean I do love him. I love him as my child's father and as my husband. I'm in love with him."

Kaine grinned and squeezed her hand. "Love him then. Don't fight it, and as his father, I'm asking you to look out for him. He thinks he's invincible. But he's human."

She wordlessly nodded and stared at the ground as he left her to sit alone. She loved Tristan, and the feeling of being in love was frightening. But she couldn't fight it. She just had to hide it to avoid the hurt she'd feel when she found out he didn't feel the same.

"There she is," Killeen said as he stood in front of the prize.

"You look lovely, sweetheart. How'd Tristan get you into bed?"

"And knock me up?" Olivia met the gaze of the man who stole her husband and forced a smile. "He's attractive, and we had been drinking. Do the math."

"He's inside sulking about you," he said, grinning. "I did that. So, you can thank me when you walk in there to find he hasn't had a single sip of alcohol. He really hates my guts, by the way."

"You've done one thing right so far," she muttered.

He laughed, shook his head and hooked his arm through hers. He had shown up unannounced and crashed a wedding he didn't even know about. The least he could do was take her back to her husband. "I like you, Olive. You're good for him."


Tristan had never known a woman so stubborn before. He knew what an idiot he was to have left her alone at their wedding. He tried making up for it, but as the end of their honeymoon neared, he had lost all hope that she'd forgive him.

However, Olivia would never admit that she had gotten over Killeen swooping in to steal her husband. She enjoyed the make-up sex too much.

"We can use our last two days to go on a cruise," Tristan offered, looking over the pamphlet as they sat on a secluded beach. "We'll dock in New York and take a flight home from there."

"Sounds great," she muttered as she continued texting Aaron. He was updating her on the patients she had to leave behind. "Or we could just go home now."

He plucked her phone away from her and hovered over her body. She could see he wasn't the least bit happy with the way he had been treated.

"I'm trying," he said, lifting her chin. It was the only way he could make her look at him. "This is supposed to be our honeymoon, and here you are barely giving two shits about the only time we will have alone. So, Olivia, I'm sorry about the wedding. I'm sorry I forced you to marry me only to—"

She kissed him on the lips and reached for the hem of his t-shirt to pull it over his head. She couldn't bear to hear him apologize for a wedding she didn't regret.

His hands moved beneath her dress where he could feel her skin on his own. "I'm sorry."

"I forgive you," she whispered, pulling him down to kiss her. "Don't regret it, Tristan."

He withdrew to see her face and choked on words when he saw the tears in her eyes. "Liv, what are you talking about?"

"The only reason why you stayed away from me after Killeen showed up was because he makes you forget you have a wife and a kid on the way." She desperately wiped her tears away, but the beating in her chest refused to settle. "You can apologize all you want for the wedding, but it still happened."

"I love you," he whispered.

She took a deep breath. "What?"

"I love you," he said louder for her to hear. "If some part of me didn't think I could, I would have denied ever knowing you. I was an ass to you and you still got the DNA test."

She laughed through her tears and allowed him to wipe them away. "I also married you."

"You did," he whispered. His lips touched hers, but he didn't kiss her yet. "And now you're stuck with me."

She smiled. "Well, I love you, too."

They were back in the presence of everyone who wanted every detail of their honeymoon. Tristan didn't know what to tell his family. It wouldn't be right to tell his mother that they hadn't done much exploring when he spent most of his time behind a locked door with Olivia.

"You should see this," Jack said, urgently rushing into the office. He slid his phone in front of Tristan and waited for his reaction.

He didn't say anything. He was perfectly impassive when he realized what the press had gotten a hold of. His honeymoon was someone else's paycheck. They had managed to capture intimate moments of him and Olivia together on the beach.

"Contact my lawyer and every company that has my wife stamped on their page," he said, fighting his voice to stay calm. "I have to call Olivia, and if my family calls, tell them to meet me at the Devereux residence."

His cell phone was already ringing when he reached for it in his pocket. Olivia's name flashed across the screen, and for a second, he panicked.

But the feeling passed when he picked up. "Hi, Liv."

"Aaron showed me already."

He could hear the smile in her voice. "You're not angry?"

"Very angry. It makes us both look bad." She paused for a moment, and Tristan could hear her talking to someone else on the line. "Aren't you going to greet your wife?"

"God, Olivia, I love you," he whispered as he left his office to take the elevator down.

He hung up and met up with Jack at the front entrance who was pushing the photographers and reporters out of the way. It wasn't common that he had the public eye on him, but when a woman on the beach with his wedding ring was involved, everyone wanted to know everything. He was used to it.

Olivia stepped out in her white pea coat and waited for her husband to approach. She was aware of the eyes on her, but she chose to ignore it when the most important thing was in front of her. "I've been thinking that maybe it's time to move."

Tristan opened the back door of the car she had arrived in and waited for her to enter first. Then he followed and immediately took her hand in his. "Where should we move?"

"Somewhere close to the Devereux home," she said, smiling at the thought. "I have a family now. And I do apologize for stealing yours, but it's new for me."

"They're all yours. You're our family. You never have to be alone."

He had said that to her once. She truly believed she'd never be alone with Tristan and their child in her life. And with a family like the Devereux one, alone wasn't a word in their vocabulary.

# Chapter 7

"I'd sell it for a little extra cash," Sadie said which only earned a blush from Olivia and a glare from Tristan.

"Do you know how inappropriate it is to be looking at pictures of your brother on the beach?" Tristan turned to Olivia when she slapped his arm. "Baby, I don't want my family seeing our intimate moments together."

She ruefully smiled at him and hugged his body close to hers. She was wearing one of his sweaters he kept in the house from high school and a pair of Victoria's jeans. She wanted to be comfortable.

"Uncle Tristan," Lana whined when he pushed the magazines to the center of the table. "How come I can't see them?"

"Because you will be at least thirty before you know what this means," Tristan said to the little girl. He was protective of her since she was the only child in the family. At least for now, she was. Soon enough he would have his own to protect. "Olivia, I have something to show you."

She took his hand and followed him down the hall, ignoring the murmurs from his family as they disappeared. Tristan opened a door and turned on a light, taking her further into the room where a polished crib sat in the corner.

"My dad used to love working in the garage," he said, admiring the crib that would hold their child. "He made this for us. I don't want to know the sex yet. I just want our baby to be ours. No labels."

"That's all I've ever wanted." Olivia kissed her husband and dropped her head against his shoulder. He was her sole comfort in moments there wasn't any.

Tristan opened his mouth to speak, but he was interrupted

when his brother walked into the room – his hands tucked into his pockets and head hung low.

"You need to come out here," Connor said. "Eloise is here."

Eloise Chase was the woman Olivia was meant to fear. She was Killeen's step sister who often came into town to visit her estranged family. It was a rare thing when she did, and Tristan knew she had only come to interrupt something. She was good at that.

Eloise stood in the foyer of the Devereux residence where her hand rested still on her protruding belly. She had sworn that the child she was carrying was Devereux blood – Tristan's blood to be exact.

"This is just perfect," Olivia murmured, shaking her head in disbelief. Everything had finally fallen into place only to be torn apart by the hands of an angry ex-girlfriend. "I need some air."

Tristan grabbed his wife's hand to keep her from leaving and pulled her to his side. "I want a DNA test then I will take responsibility when the results come back."

"You trusted her when she went to you claiming she was carrying your child," Eloise said, jabbing her thumb at Olivia.

Tristan scoffed. "The proof, Eloise. Where is it?"

"The late nights," she said, glancing that the wedding ring on his finger. "You don't remember sneaking out to the shed after dark? You wouldn't want me going to Killeen about this, would you?"

Tristan knew she wouldn't dare. Killeen hated the idea of Eloise as his sister back in high school, but Tristan knew they were each other's dirty little secret. It wasn't hard for him to figure that out when he caught them together minutes before he was expected to meet her one night. That was years ago, but he hadn't cut her off until he met Olivia.

"You won't," he said, his lips lifting into a smirk. "If you tell Killeen, I won't be the only one demanding a DNA test."

Olivia immediately broke free from Tristan's hold. The whole situation was out of her control and something she didn't want to control. Learning that her husband's on again, off again girlfriend was carrying his child was stressful enough. And hearing his girlfriend was his best friend's girlfriend and step sister was too much to handle.

Tristan caught his wife again, but she roughly pushed him away and stormed out of the kitchen.

"Liv, sweetheart, let me explain," he said, following her.

"I don't want to hear a word."

"Olivia–"

"How dare you?" She turned around to face him, tears in her eyes that she didn't bother to hide. "You obviously weren't done with her when you married me and then fucked me. You won't be done with her any time soon, and I don't want to be someone's second choice."

"Olivia," he said harshly as he backed her against the wall. "You are not a fucking choice. You're my wife, the woman I love. I'm yours. I'm only yours."

"You made me marry you when you found out this was your baby. What if she is carrying your child?"

"I don't know," he whispered, cupping her face in his hands. "But I'll figure it out. Everything will be alright."

"No, it won't." Her eyes fell shut when his mouth touched hers. They wouldn't be sharing intimate moments together anymore, and she couldn't prepare herself for that. "And I'm not going to pretend it will be fine."



There it was. Tristan Devereux shared his blood with the child growing inside of Eloise Chase. He didn't love the woman. He loved Olivia, and one week away from her had been the most painful thing to bear.

He crumpled the test results and threw it into the wastebasket before grabbing his keys. He needed to see his father who always knew what to say in situations worse than this. But first, he needed to see his wife to make sure she was doing well.

He got to her old apartment and impatiently waited on the other side of the door. Aaron answered with an exasperated sigh before inviting him inside.

"She refuses to cry over a man who just broke her heart,"

he said to Tristan, following him to Olivia's room.

"Her stubbornness is why I love her," Tristan muttered. He pushed the door open and sighed in relief when he saw the peaceful scene of Olivia fast asleep.

Her hands were protectively on her baby bump, and what Tristan really wanted to do was climb in beside her to make all his worries disappear. But leaving her be was the best option. So, he left the apartment and drove down to the old house. He had caused so much trouble there.

His father was in his study, but he welcomed his son, as if he had already known there was trouble, and poured him a glass of scotch. "Tell me, son."

So, he did. Tristan told his father everything from the affair with Eloise for so many years and then falling in love with Olivia. He didn't leave out a single detail when all he could bear to do was pour his heart out to the one man who had always gotten him out of a mess.

"I hurt Olivia," he ended with a sigh.

"I spoke to Olivia at the wedding," Kaine said, wishing he could wipe the defeated look off his son's face. He would try as hard as he possibly could. "She loved you then, and that woman sounded so sure of it even when she felt doubtful."

"When was this?" Tristan asked, suddenly intrigued to know more.

"When you left her for hours to spend time with Killeen."

"That woman has a great poker face," Tristan commented, remembering how angry Olivia was that he left even when she had been in love with him, too. "I can't leave my
wife. She means too much to me, and she's carrying my damn kid."

"So, what will you do about Eloise?"

Tristan shrugged. "You always trusted us to make our own decisions and deal with the consequences. But I'm asking you to please tell me what to do this once."

Kaine rubbed the beard across his jaw and nodded. He'd tell his son what he truly thought. "Don't let Olivia go. I don't care what it takes to keep her. We will not lose her because of one small issue at hand. And tell Eloise she can't be a bother. You will be a man and take care of her child, but remember who the woman you love is."

"Thank you, Dad." He stood up and was surprised when his father embraced him.

Kaine had always been affectionate with his children, but Tristan was never like them, which was why he appreciated Olivia. She had shaken Tristan from his tough skin and showed him the love he deserved.

"The next time you come home, bring Olivia or I will not let you into this house."

Tristan chuckled, but he knew his father was dead serious.

# Chapter 8

Olivia had woken up to the sound of pounding outside the apartment door. She checked the time on her phone only to find that it was past midnight on a Thursday evening. She felt faint as she wrapped her comforter around herself and walked to the door, checking through the peephole to find Tristan on the other side.

"What do you want?" she asked. She could see he was done fighting. But she wasn't quite yet.

"My wife. I just want my wife."

"I'm surprised you didn't marry Eloise for carrying your baby by now."

Tristan was angry. He wanted to hit something, but all he wanted was to hold his wife. Then hit something for being stupid. "It's been a long night, Liv. I just want to sleep by your side tonight."

Her heart ached. God knew she wanted him by her side, too. She didn't want to spend another night without the man she loved. But it had been two weeks, and he was now finally coming for her.

"What took you so long?" she whispered to herself.

"I don't know," he replied. She was surprised he could hear her, but the walls weren't so thick around here anyway. "I'm begging you to come home. I miss you."

"Do you still love me?"

"I can't do this behind the door. I need to see you."

Olivia reluctantly unlocked the door and stood frozen when she saw what a mess her husband had become. "You didn't come for me."

"I had to clean up," he said, dragging a hand through the disheveled mess on top of his head. "I had to figure everything out. But I love you, Olivia. I know what this must look like—"

"Do you?" Olivia blinked away the tears in her eyes, but doing so only made them fall. "From where I'm standing, it looks like I was right about you already having a soccer team of kids out there. It looks like you're going to have two children, and I don't want you to be the father to someone else's children. So pick, Tristan. Pick either me or Eloise."

"I chose you already." He shook his head. He couldn't do this. "But I pick my children. You can hate me, but I have learned to choose my family above all things. I'm not doing this with you."

She stood blinking at him for a long moment then finally said, "I'll find a lawyer first thing tomorrow morning. I don't want anything from—"

"Stop," he growled, suddenly sober from his exhaustion. "I will not let you leave me."

"I'll give you rights to your child."

"Listen to yourself, Olivia."

"You didn't choose your family," she accused. "You say you value your family, but I'm your family. And you didn't pick me."

"I have responsibilities. Eloise's child is one of them."

"Then we're done," she said, opening the door to her apartment. "Leave, Tristan."

He vigorously shook his head and stepped toward her, engulfing her trembling body in his arms. "I'm not finished with you, Liv."

"Well, I'm finished, Tristan. You wanted an heir, and now you have two of them."


Daphnia slid a plate of lunch in front of her son and sighed when he didn't look up from his cell phone. "You've lost weight, *mon petit.*"

Tristan attempted to smile and leaned over to kiss his mother's cheek. "I'm not little anymore, *mère.*"

"You're still my little boy," she said, ignoring the scowl on his face upon hearing that. "Eat because Lord knows you were stupid enough to come home without your wife. You'll need all the energy you can muster when you tell your father Olivia filed for divorce."

"She hasn't filed yet," he told his mother. "And I'll win her back before she can."

"You will win our Olive back or you really won't be able to walk in this house again."

Sadie rushed into the kitchen. Once word got out that their brother had been kicked to the curb by his wife, she couldn't believe he had messed up so quickly. And she was angry at him.

"What is all this shit about you leaving Olivia?" Sadie asked, pointing a finger at her younger brother. "Killeen is on his way over here to kill you for knocking up his sister. Why aren't you far from here trying to get your wife back?"

"Because this is all the fight I have left." Tristan took a sip of the coffee his mother set out for him and scratched his stubble down to his neck. "I need something stronger."

Stephen walked by and clamped a hand over his brother's shoulder, pushing him back onto the stool. "You will not drink her away. But I have something just as good for you."

Connor and Joseph joined the two of them in the car once they were out in the driveway. The three brothers shared a knowing look, but Tristan was staring out the window when they pulled out the driveway.


Aaron couldn't spend his weekend sitting in the house. His job was to comfort Olivia and reassure her that her life wasn't falling apart, but he also had a job to make sure she was distracted.

Olivia didn't even argue as he dragged her into his car and drove down to the bar. Of course, she couldn't drink, but Aaron knew the social scene was at least a way out of bed.

The music was loud as the two of them stepped into the bar. Drunk and dirty men whistled at the dancers on the floor, and Olivia immediately walked over to the bar to order a Sprite.

"Straight to the bar then," Aaron murmured.

"I wish it was stronger."

"Keep your head up, Olivia. We'll dance and then go home to watch a few movies. I'll even let you cry if you at least give this place a try."

Joseph recognized the auburn hair from across the room the second he returned for some drinks. He tapped Connor's shoulder and nodded toward his sister in law, scowling when he saw the man who wouldn't keep his hands off her.

"We could introduce ourselves," Connor said to his brother before glancing sideways at a distracted Tristan. "Or we could give the hopeless one another round."

"Get the fuck off," Tristan growled at the dancer.

"She's doing her job," Stephen said, giving the woman a rueful smile.

Olivia knew that mean voice from anywhere. She grew to love it and allowed her eyes to travel the bar. She saw Joseph and Connor already staring intently at her. Tristan was texting on his phone just a few feet away, and Stephen was engaged with an exotic dancer. All the Devereux brothers were there.

"We have to leave," she pleaded with Aaron.

But of course, he was oblivious to the members of her family and shook his head at her. "Ten minutes then I'll let you cry tonight."

"I gotta take a call," Tristan announced. He hadn't even recognized his own wife as he disappeared to the bathroom.

"Oh," Aaron said, finally realizing why his friend was so persistent on going home. "Your husband is here."

"And her brothers," Joseph said as he protectively pulled Olivia away from the stranger. "Olive, who is this?"

She glared at Aaron who only watched her with a smirk then turned back to the brothers. "He was at the wedding, guys. I'm fine."

Tristan came back from the restroom with a scowl on his face which only deepened when he saw Olivia. His brother had an arm around her when he approached and tucked his cell phone into his back pocket.

"I'm leaving," he said, barely acknowledging his wife. "I have a situation to deal with."

"Fuck that," Connor spat as he glared at his brother. "Your wife is standing in front of you. Fucking say something."

"It's okay." Olivia's voice was almost too small to be heard.

Tristan didn't fail to notice that her eyes were red and her face was tireless. She seemed to be well taken care of, but he didn't trust that the baby was strong enough with only a few more months left of her pregnancy. She was too weak to be properly caring for their child, and he knew it was his fault.

"Eloise has gone into labor earlier than expected," he told his brother. "I called Jack, so don't worry about me."

Olivia bit her lip to keep from crying and tried to follow him when he stormed out, but Joseph held her back. He knew that if he let her go, his brother would only hurt her more.

"Why is he doing this?" she whispered through her suppressed sobbing. "He picked her. He said he wouldn't pick, but he picked her."

"Do you need to go home?" Aaron asked, offering her a tight embrace. "We can go."

"She can come with us," Stephen offered, finally aware of the situation when he found Olivia surrounded by his brothers. "We'll take her home."

"It's okay," she assured Aaron. "I'll call you if I need anything."

Tristan had just enough with the constant texts and calls from his family. He had no control of either situation he was thrown into. He had to choose between missing the birth of his first born or leaving his wife, and he made his decision. He had a premature baby in an incubator and couldn't be bothered at the moment. He settled with shutting off his phone and kept it in his back pocket.

"You don't have to stay," Eloise said, bringing Tristan's hand to her mouth to kiss it.

But he withdrew and shook his head. "I'm leaving once you fall asleep. I'm also waiting for the DNA results."

"You got those while I was pregnant."

"Who knows what you did to keep me?" he accusingly asked. "I have a wife and a child. I'm praying your child isn't mine."

"Mr. Devereux," a nurse interrupted, handing a folded sheet of paper to Tristan. "Your results."

He quickly unfolded the paper and scanned the words. He handed her the results and crossed his arms over his chest, inhaling deeply. The air suddenly didn't feel so toxic, and his lungs were finally cleared.

"The alleged father is excluded as the biological father of the tested child." Tristan laughed but not out of humor and ran a hand through his messy hair. "Whoever the poor bastard is, let him know that I sat through hours of birth for his child. Now if you'll excuse me, I have to save a marriage you fucked up."

Tristan only had two things on his mind as he drove home where he found out Olivia would be staying for the night. One of them included being in his wife's loving arms again. And the second was their child he never in a million years thought about leaving behind.

# Chapter 9

Killeen had been sitting outside in the driveway for half an hour trying to find the courage to talk to Tristan. He wasn't angry. In fact, he felt nothing. The right thing to do in a complicated situation was to own up to any mistakes that he had made which may have contributed to the problem.

"I heard Eloise went into labor," he said as he sat beside Tristan on the porch of the old Devereaux home. "Will she be alright?"

"I fucked her," Tristan unconsciously said. "And so did you. You fucked your sister. And then she fucked me over. I suggest you take the test next."

"How'd you know?"

He took a deep breath and faced Killeen, shaking his head as he said, "I was there, Killeen. That night before I left for college, you were leaving the shed. She played us both."

"I knew her before she was even my sister. It's fucked up that I carried on with this for so long, but you know how it is."

"I do," Tristan said, nodding his head to agree. "You love her. It's wrong though."

"What'd you see in her?" he asked Tristan out of curiosity.

"You'd probably kill me if I was honest."

Killeen considerably nodded and deeply sighed into the air. "You have Olivia now. I guess I can't care what happened with Eloise."

"Good luck with everything." Tristan stood up to face the door and hesitated for a moment. "Maybe you should see her. She shouldn't be alone right now."

Then he left and made his way up the stairs where he found his old bedroom door slightly ajar. Olivia was curled up on the floor in one of his t-shirts, fast asleep. She was vulnerable and delicate, and he had hurt her.

"I'm sorry for everything," he whispered, lifting her onto his bed before stepping away to undress. "I'm so sorry, Liv."

Olivia jerked awake and stared at the face above her with wide eyes. It took her a moment to realize she wasn't in her own bedroom. "How's the baby?"

He ruefully smiled. "The child wasn't mine. I had another test done."

"And you'll probably have another test done for my baby, too," she murmured. She didn't say anything when he climbed into bed and pressed his lips to her cheek.

"We got married because of this child. I don't need a test to prove anything." He lowered his head to kiss her and deeply moaned into her mouth. It had been too long since he had felt the comfort of her arms around him and the taste of her lips in his mouth. "I ruined us, but I can fix it."

"I don't forgive you."

"I know," he whispered.

"And you made me cry. I don't cry."

"I know," he whispered again.

"You broke my heart."

"I know."

"And I'm really hurt."

"I know that, too."

"But all I want is for you to make it up to me like this," she said, grazing her fingers along the bulge pressed against her thigh. "I want you to make love to me. And I want you to pick."

He looked down at the wounded woman and grunted as he thrusted into her. He held her close to him, offering slow strokes to keep her with him for as long as he possibly could. "I do value my family. And you are my family, so I will always pick you. I'm sorry I broke your heart. I'm sorry that I hurt you. But most of all, I'm sorry that I didn't pick you."

"I can't forgive you right now." She kissed him and allowed his lips to relearn every inch of her body. Although her heart was hurting, his touch at least shut out the pain for a fleeting moment.

. . . . . . . . . . . . .

Olivia was on a runaway train. That was what Sadie had called it when she tried sneaking out of the Devereux home. She didn't stop her but never promised to keep her mouth shut if her brother asked where his wife had gone to.

Olivia had spent her last night with her husband like she wanted, but her heart was still too broken to stay. She couldn't forgive Tristan. He had broken her, and she no longer felt like they could be a family after he had abandoned her for weeks.

While her husband wasn't by her side, Olivia had taken the liberty of looking up a few of her potential parents. It wasn't easy. But after lack of sleep and a lot of crying over Tristan, she found them. Or people she was hoping were them.

Frederick and Julia Howard lived in the high end of Chicago. They owned multiple businesses that shut down just a decade ago and were retired as a couple with one daughter who collected art from all around the world.

Her phone rang in her pocket, and she slid the ignore icon when she saw it was Tristan. The Devereux household tried reaching out to Olivia in the two hours she had been gone, but she wasn't far away enough to know she was safe from them hunting her down. Finally, on the verge of breaking apart, she called Kaine.

"Olive, are you safe?" was the first thing he asked when he picked up.

"Please tell them to stop," she begged, holding in her tears. "I've left your family alone. Now leave me alone."

"Never," he whispered. "You are a blessing to this family. Wherever you are, come home so we can figure this out."

"I can't. I loved Tristan, and he took it away from me."

"I understand," he said with a sigh. "But what about the child?"

"I'll take care of my baby for the time being."

"Are you filing for divorce?"

"No," she said. "I'll be home soon. You can tell your son that."

"Tell him yourself," he said, stepping toward the train that had stopped in front of him.

Olivia hung up when she saw Kaine and Daphnia waiting on the platform. Daphnia embraced the woman first and checked every part of her face to make sure she was alright.

Tristan was still sitting on the bench – his head hung low.

"How'd you find me?" she asked no one in particular.

"Did you really think leaving the Devereuxs would be that easy?" Daphnia asked. She laughed when Olivia blushed.

"You can't leave us," Kaine told her, kissing her reddened cheek. "What are you doing here anyway?"

"I was here looking for my parents." Her breath caught when Tristan turned to look at her. "I appreciate you coming out here, but I need to do this alone."

"You never have to be alone," Tristan said. He finally stood from the bench and approached her. He was cautious, but he wasn't afraid to get close to his wife. "Olive, take me back. I hurt you, and I did things I will regret for the rest of my life. But if you leave me for people who abandoned you in the first place, I will forever regret letting you go. And I won't stop you from going because I know I shouldn't keep you away from your blood. But I'm begging you to just pick me."

She closed her eyes and shut out the world for a moment. She was back in her apartment when she begged Tristan to choose her over Eloise. He couldn't do it then, but he did last night when all was broken.

"If I do pick you," she said, blinking away her tears, "what would happen?"

Tristan snaked an arm around her waist, taking several steps to close the distance until there was no space left between them. "I'd spend forever asking for your forgiveness and forevermore earning it. I'll love you for the rest of my life and after that when we're in the afterlife together."

"I'm not sure I believe in that," she murmured.

He let a painful chuckle escape him and traced her bottom lip with his thumb. His skin against hers was all it took for her to cave. "Say you'll come home with me."

"Leave me again, and I swear to God I will really kill you, Tristan Dev–"

His lips captured hers almost in slow motion. The sweet taste of her mouth was all he needed to come to life again as he pressed her tighter against his body. Never again would he let this woman ago. Never again would he allow her to hurt.

"So, Mr. Devereux, are you taking me home?" she asked – her breath warm and ragged against his mouth. She didn't need to meet the people who abandoned her when they would never think to come looking for her. Only Tristan would do that.

"Where's that, Mrs. Devereux?"

She hummed as she fell into a deep thought and kissed him again. She was where she needed to be. "Your bedroom, preferably. But anywhere you'd like."

## ABOUT THE AUTHOR

Sheila is a college undergraduate student at the University of Minnesota – Twin Cities. Her writing first took off on Wattpad, a storytelling community online in 2014 when "The Billion Dollar Heir" was first published. Since then, she's written eight other installments for The Billion Dollar Series as well as other popular novels.

CPSIA information can be obtained
at www.ICGtesting.com
Printed in the USA
LVOW10s0106310717
543211LV00010B/709/P

9 781548 359256